PS Cottier is a poet, writer, anthologist and book reviewer who lives in Canberra. She has a particular interest in speculative poetry, having co-edited *The Stars Like Sand: Australian Speculative Poetry* with Tim Jones (IP, 2014). A short collection of poems called *Quick Bright Things: Poems of Fantasy and Myth* was published by Ginninderra Press (2016), and her poetry has appeared in Canada, England, India, New Zealand and the United States, as well as in Australia. PS Cottier was awarded a PhD for a thesis on images of animals in Dickens by the Australian National University, and she also completed a law degree in Melbourne. She has worked as a tea-lady, union organiser, university tutor and lawyer, but now writes full time. *Monstrous* is her fifth collection of poetry.

Interactive Press
Brisbane

Monstrous

PS Cottier

Interactive Press

Interactive Press
an imprint of IP (Interactive Publications Pty Ltd)
Treetop Studio • 9 Kuhler Court
Carindale, Queensland, Australia 4152
sales@ipoz.biz
http://ipoz.biz/

Printed in 12 pt Baskerville on 14 pt Avenir Book.

ISBN: 9781922332172 (PB); 9781922332189 (eBk)

NATIONAL LIBRARY OF AUSTRALIA

a catalogue record of this book is available
from the National Library of Australia

for Nick, who tolerates gnomes

'As phantoms frighten beasts when shadows fall.'

– Dante Alighieri, *Inferno*

Acknowledgements

Book design: David P. Reiter

Front cover image: Zoe Hartland

Author photo: Geoffrey Dunn

The section of the Frankenstein sequence entitled "The creature runs through the Arctic ice, pursued by Dr Frankenstein" was published in *Cordite 91*, April 2019, ed. Nathan Curnow.

"The Ashes, 3150 A.D." was published in *Eye To The Telescope*, Issue 32, USA, April 2019, ed. Lisa Timpf. Republished in *The Cricket Society News Bulletin*, No. 597, UK, July/August 2019, ed. John Symons.

"The fruit of her hands" was published in *Midnight Echo*, No 11, April 2015, ed. Kaaron Warren.

"The backcomber" appeared in the poet's blog, pscottier.com

"Lycium barbarum" was published in *Umbel & Panicle*, Issue 5, Nightshade themed edition, October 2017. Included in *The Rhysling Anthology*, USA, 2018, ed. Linda D. Addison.

"Freckles" was published in *Sponge*, Issue 5, New Zealand, 2019, ed. Lucy-Jane Walsh.

Contents

Introduction

I first came across the work of PS Cottier when she submitted a poem to *Midnight Echo*, a horror fiction magazine I was guest-editing. I'd seen a lot of poetry by then, most of it in the vein of graphic imagery and extreme adjectives. I had three files: Yes, No, Maybe. There were plenty in the No and the Maybe files; PS Cottier's poem was the first in the Yes file. It should really have been in a file all its own, called Hell Yes, that's how much I loved "The fruit of her hands". From the opening two lines 'She pulls the thin wire through — no need for a needle' to the last line (I will leave you to discover that for yourselves) I was entranced, sickened, inspired and horrified.

You can't ask for much for than that.

With PS Cottier, you do get more, though. You get her sharp, biting wit. It can be subtle, it can be more hilariously obvious, but it is always clever. Double-meanings concealing truer meanings, twisted phrases, hints.

Take this, from "Hideous whimsy: A garden of gnomes":

> Dubious, concrete glee
> must be maintained,
> batch after hatted batch.

And the glorious joy that is "The garden gnomes of the GDR lasted longer than the country", which makes me chuckle with glee every time I read it. "Mouthing off" is the same but more so; this poem is HILARIOUS and utterly terrifying at the same time. Every line is a shining gem; I would say this is one of my favourites in the book, although all the work is top notch.

Having heard and seen PS Cottier read her work, I can see her smile through this, her glancing at the audience sidelong to see if her jokes have struck home. They always strike home.

This is a poet filled with glee, with grue, with dark and light. She is remarkable in her originality and in her ideas, brilliant in her way with words and quite terrifying. She knows her stuff, both in poetical forms and in horror fiction, meaning she can play with both beautifully. Her Frankenstein suite is marvellous, not a re-telling but a re-visioning, breathing new life into this much-loved story.

There is the precision in “The King of Eyes”:

> His crown has fifty-two spikes,
> and each boasts an eye
> gouged from conquered realms,
> or scooped like a four-minute egg
> from every defeated pretender.

And the epic scope and humour of “A steam-engine to the moon”.

Monstrous is a collection to be enjoyed, delighted in, disturbed by and greatly admired.

– Kaaron Warren

1.

'Impressed upon me even more deeply': Reflections of the creature

A sequence of poems based on *Frankenstein; or, The Modern Prometheus* by Mary Shelley

The creature runs through the Arctic ice, pursued by Dr Frankenstein

What have these blunt fingers touched
what made this heart beat faster

in the flesh chest that grew it?
Before they became mine: became

the motley coat that is me?
Did this palm stroke softer flesh

in reciprocal love? My hands
(if mine they be through mere possession)

may turn black from the kiss of frost.
Even these broad splayed toes

propelling me through snow.
My flesh spreads away from itself,

as if it too finds the latticework
of my woven skin disgusting.

He chases me now, a blind dog
chained to me by loathing.

Yet he sewed these fingers
with his own. These toes he assayed

as a surveyor uses an alidade
to map continents, or mere streets.

He loved the precious detail,
retracts himself from the whole,

and would smear me on the ice.
Me, the only one ever born

without a mother, made
by pure scientific fumbling.

And so we run. Always north.
This sharpened North

tears my skin with teeth
always all its own. My own teeth

tasted flesh I never saw;
this tongue may speak languages

that even he can't speak.
I am the king of second-hand

The prince of second-feet.

A vision from the future appears to the creature as he runs

Vacanti's mouse

The nude mouse grows
a human ear on its back,
seeded with a herd of
cartilage cow cells.
Is the mouse still a mouse
carting this foreign flap
elephantine on its spine?
Does the person who
wears the cowmouseear
listen for the rampage
behind the rhubarb of chat?
If she chews gum,
does a rumen erupt
inside, like Ripley's
puissant alien?
Monstrous the tales
for such an ear;
Monstrous the listening.

Every sound an echo of an echo
straining to hear a progenitor.

The creature sees a projection of moving pictures upon the ice,
in which another monster appears.
He begins to understand that he is immortal.

The rough beast reaches Bethlehem every day, and Calvary, too

He wears metal
pushed through skin;
difference imprinted, nay,
sculpted into him;
subtle as a railway.

The monster's bolts
to receive electricity
were implanted there
in 1931. Etymologically
apt, the makeup man's
name was Jack Pierce.

This creature is Saint Sebastian,
pierced by too little love.
A second coming,
nails driven into neck,
not hands; this original
replicant, continually reborn.

This creature, begotten son of science,
and a woman called Mary,
(born of her unseen mother Mary)
is constantly betrayed.
Constantly crucified.
An echo of an echo.

This is the bolt that Jack built.
This is the neck, pierced

by knowledge,
his skin a book beyond mere tattoo;
impressed...even more deeply.
Print, skin, and hot metal are one.
He rises again and again,
resurrected by celluloid.

He is found wanting by the court,
the Hollywood court of beauty;
is hoisted again in 3D.

I am this same monster
of thick tongue and poor diction,
stumbling through an electric world.

Escape is never a possibility.
You read me into being again
as you hold this thin, icy book.

Read my footprints;
the impression lingers.

Freed from the constraints of time, the creature composes a new ending to the novel.

An extract from Robert Walton's last letter

Like that other Shelley's
Ozymandias, we found him frozen,
an ice statue of Dr Frankenstein,
complete, from the waist down.
Head and chest
removed, some say,
by a polar bear.
And yet, the cut so neat,
as if a cultured hand
held a surgeon's knife,
rather than the rude gape
of ravenous bear.
Inside the stomach
(and this must not be told
for reasons of propriety –
my dear sister must be kept
from this last Arctic letter)
a single finger, broad, curled
into the likeness of a foetus.
Pregnant, then, with what he authored,
two legs stood amongst the
vast and irregular plains of ice.
Two prints lead away, and
those were not the paws of
white bear, or lost bear brown.

We followed the prints
into the pages of snow
until only unpressed white remained.

Notes

The quotation in the sequence's title 'Impressed upon me even more deeply' is from Chapter 13 of *Frankenstein*.

'Vast and irregular plains of ice' in "An extract from Robert Walton's last letter" is from Chapter 3 of *Frankenstein*.

2.

Hideous whimsy: A garden of gnomes

The belly of the gnome

Round not because of ale,
not because of bratwurst,
but with a growing egg.
Like platypus, like echidna,
all young gnomes hatch.
Dubious, concrete glee
must be maintained,
batch after hatted batch.
The layer is always a he.
His stomach splits like a smile;
egg drops onto merry boots.
Overnight, the wound will heal,
the youngster breaks the shell
with a handy tool – spade or rake.
Some ask the frogs they ride on
to kick the shell into submission.
Some tunnel out with pipes,
as they are born to tobacco,
or its cuter accoutrements.

Those who see the process
have never lived to tell,
but are found, clutching chests,
as if their hearts were gnomes,
also anxious to explore.
Convenient toadstools provide
solutions for the gnomes,
salves that cause hearts to flutter,
flutter, flop and stop.

I sip my wine so cautiously.
I know the gnomes will come.

The garden gnomes of the GDR lasted longer than the country

This one looks at me sadly, remembering the caress of the probably imaginary Stasi member who owned him.

I am obviously a poor substitute, as he seems more thoughtful than when I received him from Germany (the one that still exists) via Etsy.

Nearly all his paint is gone, and he has a hole in his hand, which used to hold a spade, or a pipe, or even a rifle, as hunting gnomes are not unknown.

I have never seen a gnome posing with a dead deer, although they are given to riding squirrels and toads or leaning on mushrooms like a rotund, ugly Marlene Dietrich, if I may be forgiven for twisting the image of the tall, blonde, elegant woman associated with lamplight into gnome-hood, like the tall vase I tried to make once on a wheel that collapsed into a groaning heap.

I am not putting a spade, a rake, or a rifle, through the hole in his hand. As I am a decadent poet, I may put some ironic poem on a stick though the hole. A short one, maybe a haiku about gnomes, communism, and how he feels naked given most of his paint has gone, but I haven't had time to write it yet.

This gnome is valuable to me, so he doesn't see much of the front garden, except for the occasional airing.

On an occasional airing, he was stolen.

I just received a postcard from him in Thuringia, the region of Germany in which he was made, although, interestingly, the GDR dissolved 'States' such as Thuringia in the early 50s and Thuringia was only reborn once Germany was reunified. You weren't expecting education, were you? The postcard shows a gnome very similar to my gnome, but this one is in much better condition, and boasts a rake inserted through the hole in his hand. I find the predictability of this implement disappointing.

The postcard is in English. It says:

I enjoyed my stay in your capitalist country, but not so much as socialism.

This is confusing, but perhaps my gnome was kept in a box, or a case, or some other receptacle from, say, 1985 until quite recently when he was discovered, photographed and sold on Etsy, and he does not yet realise that the GDR no longer exists and that all Germany is capitalist? There was a film a bit like that a while back, although it was about a woman, not a gnome.

Is there a German, even a gnome, who has not heard the words 'Angela Merkel'?

And how did he know Canberra was 'capitalist', given I lounge around the garden writing poems and feeding the parrots, like a vegan version of Marx's vision of Communist 'man': '…in communist society…nobody has one exclusive sphere of activity but each can become accomplished in any branch he wishes, society regulates the general production and thus makes it possible for me to do one thing today and another tomorrow, to hunt in the morning, fish in the afternoon, rear cattle in the evening, criticise after dinner, just as I have a mind, without ever becoming hunter, fisherman, herdsman or critic.' That is from *The German Ideology*, which does not, so far as I recall, mention gnomes. It's meatier than I remember. Perhaps I should have made a clay bratwurst and inserted it in my gnome's hole.

I miss my gnome. I miss his hideous whimsy. I miss the curl of his fist with the beckoning hole through which I never threaded a flag with a poem, let alone that imaginary sausage.

Come back, gnome, and I shall give you a flag with a hammer and sickle! But first I shall have to buy it on Etsy from somewhere in Thuringia.

Every night in your garden (a gentler vision)

We overturn gnomes
to excavate magic oil –
hats spellbreaker drills.

The oil produces
only wonder and glitter –
such cool emissions.

We flip the gnomes back
onto their booted red feet.
They chug cups of oil.

Resourceful gnomes rest,
transform to painted concrete –
quiet limestone dreams.

Gnome-opticon

The judges of normality are present everywhere.
– *Michel Foucault,* Discipline and Punish

Gnome-opticon or gnomopticon – no matter.
A wheelbarrow, boasting four garden gnomes,
back to back, with a space-sliver
between them, braced on thick air.
Wherever you stand, peeping from behind trunks,
pretending to be a sparrow, or an aviary canary,
you can see them. More to the point,
they can see you, with their eight merry eyes,
allegedly merry, if merry be a side-step from misery.
They radiate enforced jollity, their eyes
count out glee like coins, more Molière's miser
then Molly Bloom's passionate yes.
One holds a spade, the better to bury.
One a rake, to gather souls into mulch.
A fisherman is third, angling for children.
One does nothing, just leers and stares.

Somewhere between fairy and clown
with their chiselled smiles – cheeks ruddy as measles.
Glance at them quickly, and look away.
Note the red tights, as if an old-school golfer putted in gore.

Their implements, poised. They watch you, watching.
They know your flickering, evasive eyes
are nervous experimental frogs, twitching and epileptic.
Graveyard jolly, carnival true, they plait a tightrope,
a tightrope of nerves, and jump upon it.
They grin and flourish their tools.
Gnomes never die, and a shadow in our heads
demands that we render them cute as treacle,
or pay tribute to unease with a thick glob of humour.
The zombie gnome. The drear permanence felt

and transmuted. The nude gnome with wee cock,
when our well-being is dismembered.

Angels weep to see the grim whimsy.
Bury these four in the barrow, and they'd pop up,
not Lazarus, not Jesus, no, by no means.
They are more like fungi, upon which other gnomes lean.
If you look over, and believe that they are simply cute,
you have fallen to their noxious brightness,
that toxic glare of fun. Pick up a shovel.
Feel your legs growing hose, your brain solidifying.
Step up. Smile. The barrow beckons.

The smell of the garden gnome

Very few lean down and sniff
their bodies, heavy as hangovers.
Hint of durian, swig of whisky,
rotten tulip bulb, ruptured haggis,
congealed blood sausage,
all these dwell under tincture
of pale pink rose,
plucked in summer and boiled.
But the turnip stink is more cat-litter
than catnip, and will wriggle in
to the quiet caverns of your nose,
hatching immortal worms of smell.
You will pray for anosmia.
Butterflies have nothing to do with it.
Moths never sleep on gnomes.

3.

Sundry monsters

Starshark

He cruises the black, supping on suns
as if they were surfers' knees.
In with the yellow or red, and out
with the black, all energy plucked
like sumptuous fruit.

His burps are meteors, his farts
destroy myriad worlds.

Of course, once your sun
is engulfed like a burning Jonah,
there are no more worries
about climate change,
to look on the bright side,
which will be impossible.

Starshark is an innocent,
has no choice in regarding stars
as so many radioactive oranges.
Erect all the nets you wish.
Bombs brush off that atomic skin
like insipid mosquitos.

Starshark cruises the heavens,
all become as beaches in northern New South Wales,
but there's no-one to blow a whistle.
The rips in the galaxies
flow around him like dreams.
Starshark's paths are never pinned by flags.

If the sun shows upside down V,
it's being eclipsed by a dorsal fin.
That's the last thing you'll ever see,
before Starshark's eternal, night-bringing grin.

Mouthing off

She's a shark, you know, a tiny one,
armed with milk teeth and coins.
She severs fingers, not legs,
hiding in lawnmowers, which she stops,
until an enquiring hand reaches
to unblock the green-clogged blades.
She strikes, starts the engine,
and the dumb machine gets the blame.
No-one sees her flying off with the digit –
they mistake her sharp chortle for canaries,

the rattle of a hula hoop of surplus teeth
is heard as a cicada's solo. She shimmies,
perched on a convenient tree,
and tucks into her well-earned, self-saucing snag.
Delightfully light, she flits on,
gathers a few more teeth, threads them,
bites a few puppies, enjoys the way
that the local pitbulls get the flak.
Her original teeth were removed long ago
in a futile attempt to stop her munching
on fingers, toes, and pets like candy.
She moved into kiddies' teeth;
a penny there, then a dollar or a Euro.
She enjoys endless, free-market chomping,
glueing a new set every Sunday,
formed from that sweet, calcium-rich bandolier.

If a knife misses carrot
and finds flesh, it is surely
our invisible sprite who abbreviates the hand.
Carpenters have felt a sudden
blunting of their grip as 'a chisel slipped',
but the wound is surprisingly multi-edged.
A tiny rose of white thorn-petals removed

the formerly useful pointer, or mere pinkie,
if it was only time for a hasty snack.

Just recently, she has diversified,
depositing a few teeth into the ears
of children who put them under pillows,
investing in her profession's future.

They dream of fingers. They dream of wings.

Leg room

Yes, the door was red,
red as a clown with a nose-cold,
and the mat outside clotted
with sticky islets of blood,
flicked there in the moments
when the entrance was open
and the legs still bled.

This is where he stowed them –
the legs of women wearing shoes
far too red for modesty,
those who danced too much,
smoked, drank and partied,
and enjoyed the unseemly sound
of their own rosy laughter.

All had their self-written joy
abbreviated by sudden punctuation
of axe – sharpest editor,
marking the text of their bodies
with their own red ink,
irrevocably shortened,
corrected and shattered.

Limbs were piled inside like wood,
and he smiled to think
of those who survived.
They now walked stiffly on wood,
their shameless shimmies
no longer seen in the market,
or polluting the innocent green.

He was supplementing the pile
with the right and left legs
of an old biddy called Sally,

caught wearing a red shawl,
which matched thigh-high boots,
dancing a tango and holding a cat
that wore a flagrant jacket and hat.

He went to throw the limbs,
found that they adhered to his hands;
sticky thin echoes of his hard work.
He put the feet under his own boots –
such a sensible brown –
and stomped to remove them,
frowning at the inconvenience.

He hit his head on the wall,
so solidly built of silencing stone.
Dizzy, he fell towards the pile,
expecting a soft landing,
but the legs had shifted –
each standing on the bright shoe
that had attracted his ire.

But how can a severed leg kick?
he thought, as the blood-red
stiletto of the young girl called Kim
made contact with his left temple
as if to propel his head
between the posts of an unseen goal.
It swung back on nothing.

His head swelled like a bulb,
about to bloom, as a centipede
formed of all the legs,
as they can-canned past him.
Each one made perfect contact
with chin, eye, or cheek,
jaw, ear, or fast-flattening nose.

He could not stand,
seemed to have stuck
on the floor, just as Sally's limbs

still adhered to his hands.
The others kicked, but the bones
of the biddy drove themselves deep
inside the cracked room of his skull.

Some say the legs returned to their owners –
a procession of the abbreviations.
Not true, say I, for every fine evening,
before the women dance, they bow,
remember those pruned, years ago,
by the Woodman and his Axe.
Surely they bow to the lame or the dead?

Yet, it's true that the young lass called Kim,
decked in purple and crimson,
is dancing tonight, swirling, spinning,
a regular planet of glee.
And Sally, ancient as any lost tale,
and an elegant cat, are purring,
tapping, and teaching the tango.

Freckles

Some may call them summer-spots, but they are not,
although they may manifest themselves when the sun
bakes us into compliance. Each freckle is a small drawing,
carefully inked while we doze, indicating what will grow,
eventually, and take wing. If our eyes were keen enough,
microscopically adept, we might decipher the tiny glyphs.
This one is Pegasus, but Pegasus with a shedding disease
rendering him far less than bird, just a disappointing pony.
He will clip-clop through predictable, grimy suburban dreams,
paddocks of misery dragging after him like a poxy peacock's train.
That one, on that exposed shoulder, is a full Brexit of portraiture,
disastrous, yet achingly slow. The creature it represents
lurks in the future, almost recognisable as someone we once knew,
but different, different in the way a beer-glass distorts,
screaming like Munch's bloke crossed with a fairground clown.
We will meet him, surely, in an alley, late one glassy Friday night.

Who does the inking? Some say it is an alien, armed,
or an octopus, clutching a tool in each convenient tentacle.
Personally, I believe that each spot is injected by a cockroach,
taking revenge for all the traps, all that kitchen-laid pain.
The freckles will birth themselves into air: tiny puppies,
whelped into the future, sucking on fear and disgust.
There is no escape from the skin-maps, pointing where they will.
Our noses detect the provenance, painting air a clutching brown.
Far from cute, further from lovely's farthest shores,
our skin itches with a colony of a thousand pregnant clouds.

The backcomber

Her hair is coiffured once a month.
Though she goes to bed unkempt,
glamour descends like a dream.
A scissored were-poodle inflicts revenge
for ridiculous, hedgy trims,
those uncouth bubbles of fur he wore,
imposed without his will.
She awakes to a memory of spray
and a beehive, tall as any tower.
Next month's moon may well mean quiff.
Next month's moon may just mean mullet.

The King of Eyes

His crown has fifty-two spikes,
and each boasts an eye
gouged from conquered realms,
or scooped like a four-minute egg
from every defeated pretender.
The eyes look out at courtiers,
at advisers, open and shameless
as any necessary lie.
Crowns parade around heads,
each decoration a soldier,
so there is always an eye,
or a platoon of eyes
upon you, heavy as an official chain.

We lucky, or unlucky, few
often in His Majesty's presence
have noted that he arranges
the eyes to a distinct pattern,
blue following modest brown,
and every tenth eye is green.
Opalescent eyes, beflecked,
break the pattern near each ear,
as if to drop colourful rumour
direct into the regal brain.
Some say that it is possible
for each crown-eye to wink,
and that such a wink is deadly
as any guillotine, for the flicker
is only bestowed on those
whose own eyes will soon adorn
the King's most puissant head.
I cannot say if this is true,
as I have yet to see an eye
that still sports a gown of lash.
We walk quietly around

the regal panopticon,
just in case the eyes still see,
and the King might catch the
slightest flicker of disloyalty.

Yesterday I noticed an eye
of a near emerald green
that clearly broke the pattern –
and I recognised the glance
of the King's courtesan,
who was strangely absent
from her stool near the window,
where she often sat, weaving.
I have clutched her in love,
these six months past,
and could not strangle a shudder
to see such beauty displaced.
If the eyes see, they saw me blanch,
at the elevation of her eye
from our shared soft pillow
to mere metallic display.

I am called to a meeting at eight.
My eye, such an average brown,
may yet be raised to the crown.

The fruit of her hands

'She maketh herself coverings of tapestry...'
– Proverbs 31:22 *KJV*

She pulls the thin wire through –
no need for a needle.
The skin yields, as if in love,
to this elaborate piercing,
and bones provide the loom.
Her right hand boasts lines
unreadable by any palmist:
mute poems of perfect scansion.
A pattern of virtue, she sews,
always with her plain left hand.
Now she wears a mesh glove,
painted with liquid ruby,
which slides to the floor –
ankles wear sudden scarlet.
Her lap dog tastes abundance.

Lycium barbarum

It worked like magic, and you can't say
we didn't warn them. Each goji berry
looks like a wolf's tooth, blood-soaked,
pulled by who knows what savage dentist,
spat out and dried and put into the palm
of those who would be oh-so-healthy.
And now they arise, those who would
gobble our wolfberries, and they howl
and turn upon their fellow healthnuts,
and it's all Hobbesian tooth and jowl,
and manicures morphing to paws.

I wondered if they would have scoffed so much
if we had used the name wolfberry for our product?
But Barry – our pack-leader – just howled with glee.
Never underestimate (he said) the stupidity
of those with too much time and money.
Never waste your pity on the wealthy.
They deserve to suffer first wolf problems.

The Ashes, 3150 A.D.

It's a far bigger urn than the one
that marked Australia v. England
all those long years ago.
Cricket isn't cricket,
the purists often say,
but they've been saying that
forever, give or take.
The ball still swings or spins,
and there is still a wicket,
bails awaiting collision,
and eleven men a side.
Eleven men, or beings.
But a draw is no longer an option,
and then there's that urn,
that larger urn, to be
filled with the ashes
of the loser's planet,
proudly displayed in a cabinet
at Lords. (Lords is
an artificial planet,
accessible only to those in ties,
or twinsets fit for a Queen.)
Gravity makes a difference,
as do the umpires,
armed with far more than fingers,
as they adjudicate
on the sweet green fields of fear.

4.

A steam-engine to the moon

edited by PS Cottier

Editor's Introduction

This introduction contains spoilers, and should be read after the poem that follows.

This short, strange, anonymous manuscript was found in an antique suitcase in the attic of a house in Sydney in 2016. The owner of the house, who also wishes to remain anonymous, passed it onto me, as he knows I have an interest in the literature of the nineteenth century.

I have decided to take the opportunity to include it alongside my own poems about monsters. Firstly, the work seems to be something of a traveller's guide to the near monstrous excesses of the nineteenth-century English colonial mind, as epitomised by the writer of the poem. The presence of aliens perceived to be evil in the poem (or, to be accurate, the narrator's belief that he came near to such creatures) adds another portion of monster to the mix.

From the first reading, I had little doubt that the excursion described in train-track rhyming couplets (if train-tracks can be of somewhat uneven length) must be fictitious. Apart from physics rendering such a project impossible, no such event could have taken place without considerable publicity, and articles in the press. While Facebook and its ilk may not yet have been invented, numerous newspapers were in existence in the nineteenth century, and no expedition to the moon could have been organised, let alone mounted, without journalists being aware, and documenting the momentous event.

Similarly, later expeditions to the moon have revealed no evidence of previous human contact, and no doubt remnant gnomes and British flags would have been described and retrieved by American astronauts, or detected by satellites and/or later landings of unpeopled craft. (Unless, of course, we have all indeed been 'prey to magicians', as the poet has it in this work, in the 1960s as well as the nineteenth century, and no-one has actually ever visited the moon. Many still hold to this view.)

The manuscript is obviously unfinished, with numerous leaps and omissions detectable. For example, the launch of the vessel is not directly described (despite a passing reference to 'thrust');

surely a major omission, although the process of obtaining a ticket is depicted at some length. Major gaps in the manuscript are indicated by asterisks.

The brief time described on the moon itself is entirely taken up with imperialistic display, although, interestingly, garden gnomes are also described; creatures that, like Prince Albert, found their way to England from Germany in the mid-nineteenth century. More on gnomes below.

The section dealing with cogs, which contains the immortal words 'with clanking clanks, and whirring whirls!' appears on a separate piece of paper sandwiched into the journal in which the manuscript is written. It is interpolated into the text near where the orphan leaf was found.

Another included piece of paper includes an (almost) alphabetical list of industries undertaken in Victorian Britain and its colonies, beginning with Asbestos mining and ending with Zinc mining. Fortunately, the poet did not move on to include these industries in the work itself, possibly due to the difficulties in efficiently extracting sufficient rhyme. Careful analysis of the list might result in a more accurate date for the writing of the poem, or at least the list itself, as it cannot be said that it was necessarily written at the same time as the rest of the work.

This List of Industry may have been intended to be included in the poem in the section including the lines 'Our moon may prove to be another Bombay,/Or Peking, or Manchester, and who shall say nay?' but no indication is given. It was inserted at the extreme back of the journal. After some internal debate, I decided not to include the list, as it contains nothing undiscoverable by Google.

As a relatively early work of science fiction, the poem has some interest. (Of course, outliers such as Cyrano de Bergerac wrote of travels to the moon centuries before this work, but it was still written well before most such literature appeared.)

Similarly, as a record of the limitations of the poet (and I use that word loosely) it may provide the reader with some amusement. His imperialistic view of England's right to colonise, his inability to see women as anything but 'fair nymphs' and weak, and his unthinking acceptance of class divisions, will immediately be apparent, as will his surprisingly modern over-attachment to the exclamation mark.

The passage relating to noises overheard coming from a locked cabin, which may, in the poet (and/or narrator's) view, belong to creatures from another planet, raises the tantalising prospect that the alleged mission to the moon was in fact due to extraterrestrial assistance, a possibility that seems not to have occurred to the narrator himself. (It is also apparent that the voices of the assumed aliens are quite similar to the description of the ship's cogs.) Psychoanalytically, it is interesting that the narrator is searching for a woman when he overhears the incomprehensible babble of monsters, which renders him 'pregnant'.

The reference to terrorism, in the alleged train-ship being destroyed by 'Luddites' (a group for whom Byron felt some sympathy), before the moon is turned into an industrial site, also speaks to modern concerns of terrorism, and, perhaps more significantly, to the earth's climate being threatened by the emissions of industry. (That the terrorism described briefly in the poem occurred at Salisbury, the cathedral town now associated with a more modern type of terrorism, provides another point of interest to the poem, which was not detectable when I first read the manuscript in 2016.)

It is also notable that the poet seemingly describes Ada Lovelace without admitting to any knowledge of the real identity of the character Jane Gordon, which will strike the modern reader immediately, at least if they have any knowledge of computers, feminism, or Byron.

Is the poet in fact less limited than the poem's narrator, in deliberately inserting Lovelace in this work without any explanation? I leave such speculation to the reader. At least Ada's dates are well known, 1815-1852, and, from the description given by the admittedly unreliable poet, she is young at the time of the alleged expedition, which would perhaps give a date no later than 1847 in which to place this work of the imagination. The useful reference to 'Her Majesty' gives an earliest date of June 1837, as Queen Victoria ascended to the throne on the 20th of that month.

This tentative date ties in reasonably well with the presence of gnomes, first introduced into England from their German homeland in the 1840s, although their heyday was somewhat later. For more information about gnomes, the reader is referred to Twig Way's excellent book *Garden Gnomes: A History* (Oxford: Shire Publications, 2009).

It is possible that the poet himself believed that he actually undertook his journey. On the other hand, references to mental illness ('*lunar*tics', 'poor Richard Dadd') may in fact indicate that the poet knows that belief in such a technologically impossible journey would require a kind of mental incapacity. (I would not condone the poet's equating mental illness with notions of intellectual incapacity, but the work was written long before more nuanced views of living with mental illness existed in the wider community.)

The opening quotation from Byron's *Don Juan* appears in the original manuscript. (That inclusion must surely provide some indication that the poet deliberately describes Ada Lovelace, Byron's daughter, in the work.)

More McGonagall than Byron, the lunar steam-engine has found its way out of the suitcase, and into the world.

– PS Cottier, PhD
Canberra, 2020

Byron, *Don Juan*, Canto X

1

When Newton saw an apple fall, he found
In that slight startle from his contemplation –
'Tis said (for I'll not answer above ground
For any sage's creed or calculation) –
A mode of proving that the earth turned round
In a most natural whirl, called gravitation;
And this is the sole mortal who could grapple,
Since Adam, with a fall or with an apple.

2

Man fell with apples, and with apples rose,
If this be true; for we must deem the mode
In which Sir Isaac Newton could disclose
Through the then unpaved stars the turnpike road
A thing to counterbalance human woes;
For, ever since, immortal man hath glowed
With all kinds of mechanics, and full soon
Steam-engines will conduct him to the moon.

A steam-engine to the moon

The ticket was parchment, rolled tight
delivered a full month before the flight,

illuminated, as if by ancient monk's hand,
(although the firm's offices are on The Strand).

I unrolled this, my most precious cigar,
that would take me up, and take me so far

as if I were smoke breathed into the sky,
rewriting the meaning of the word 'high'.

The most glorious invention of the age!
The engineer's genius, and the Sage

unknown who had set his strong will
Lord Byron's fleeting vision to fulfil,

and aim, within five years, if not sooner,
to design a railway fully lunar.

The scoffers scoffed, as scoffers do,
but the Sage (would that I knew just who!)

pushed on and laid first plan, then track,
to ensure both the up, and then bringing back.

To plan, to weigh, to figure, design,
to weld, to furnish, to power and to find

resources and men and steel and tin,
and how to keep sweet air within,

and space without, despite its knocking,
the physics of which were most shocking,

or so I've heard, for mathematics and I
are further away than moon and sky,

through which the welded tracks now reach,
and that moon turning, cheese or pale peach,

waiting for eager mortal mouth,
and mechanical fingers, launched far south.

***

The manifestation of human brain,
encased in emphatic form of Train.

I have a ticket! And before she wanes,
she'll never know loneliness again,

but be most thoroughly explored,
her plains measured, her minerals bored,

or at least sampled, one at a time
(for prospecting comes before the mine).

My feet will be there in the dust
and the rest of me, with wanderlust,

not quite heroic, nor yet Byronic,
but a lunar excursion may prove a tonic

for one who once knew dearer faces
and longs for distracting, unfamiliar places

and the sight of the earth from the moon
will assuredly lift my habitual gloom.

***

The ticket cost me £10,000; substantial!
But access was not secured by mere financials.

A list was made of those with the means
willing to pay, and of the fifteen,

a ballot was held, and out came my name!
(First time I ever had luck in a game.)

And now I hold this most wond'rous cigar
that will take me to the moon, if not the stars.

***

Cogs bloomed like marigolds,
brass marigolds, bright and bold

turning; so may little worlds,
with clanking clanks, and whirring whirls!

Organs of celestial motion!
Pure science! Not witches' potions.

Such strong, metallic potency!
Heart of our mechanical century!

Glowing, turning little suns;
magic webs of power are spun.

***

I see no steam, just many stars outside,
which one day we may also bestride!

To think of all those who've wondered
about these lights amongst which we wander!

***

A small porthole showed her, just as round
as that framing window, and a grating sound

of brakes, I assumed, assailed my ears.
I tightened the straps, hoped that the gears

and cogs were working just as they should,
my lack of knowledge as heavy as wood,

heavy as the massive beam, brass-shot,
at which the leather formed an inextricable knot

to keep me, the traveller, safe in my seat
(a similar strap ran down to my feet).

Although I'm not given to fanciful imagery
(I'll leave that to poetesses so often shimmery),

that similar restraints are used in asylums
occurred to me, and I found myself smiling

to think that we might be called true *lunar*tics
strait-jacketed, tied to enormous sticks

with the flimsy walls of the ship as our cell,
blackness all round us, deep as a well.

We are off with the fairies like poor Richard Dadd
seeing wild visions, and totally mad,

propelled by mechanics beyond bedlam dreams,
knowing not how, nor what science means

but chasing desire like a teaspoon a lump –
my reflections were stopped by a muffled thump,

far less than I'd thought, the moment we reached
the once virginal surface, her whiteness breached

by Englishmen determined, taking big strides
with one inexplicable woman hitching a ride.

The nineteenth century after our Lord.
(I wonder why they let her aboard?)

and the moon is ours, to know and to colonise
it was enough to bring a quick tear to my eyes!

My servant came to unstrap the straps,
to remove the buckles from the brown chaps.

My hands first were freed, then lower limbs,
and, in a moment of feeling, I shook hands with Jim.

We've made it! I cried, the moon is around us!
(The porthole showed, it's true, little but dust).

Jim nodded and looked full far from hottish,
(I may record that my servant was Scottish).

He informed me that drinks were to be served
and left the cabin without further word.

Odd fellow, I thought, and then the thought passed
as I rushed to the salon to empty a glass.

The thirteen assembled, including myself,
twelve staunch men, one charming elf,

or fairy, of goodly looks, sipping champagne,
showing little of the dire mental strain

that such an excursion must produce in a woman.
Such a dilemma that she has been put in!

And she saw me, and frowned, and looked away.
It seems she was feeling somewhat distrait.

I unrolled a paper I had long since prepared
and burst into song. The composition that I shared?

My rewriting of *Jerusalem*, by William Blake,
updated for our mission's dear sake:

And do our feet
in modern times
fly from England's ancient hills?
And is Elysium to be found
upon this fair white lunar ground?

Thus I began, but strange! no soprano
joined in, no hands made the piano

sing with me, so my song somehow died,
before the last line about justified pride.

Perhaps my companions were of feebler fibre?
They were as to whisky just water or cider,

or champagne as sipped by our fairer companion
Whose laughter scented the air like roses or jasmine

though to the captain she talked mathematics!
A proposition so plainly fantastic

that I thought that the journey had affected me too.
My brain must be dizzy, my hearing askew.

But no way the oak shall bend like bamboo!
Weakness, I thought, be away with you!

Soon my sprits rose, my doubts disappeared.
Tomorrow the surface; destiny neared!

(Though the captain informed us that men would prepare
some attractions for us, and first try the piped air.)

But to bed on the moon, the earth seems her satellite,
to the teeming millions down there I sent a goodnight!

***

We are diving onto the moon, if you see what I mean,
with helmets by the brothers Charles and John Deane.

Huge tanks of air follow, and allow us to breathe
to walk and explore, without visiting Lethe.

The brain may say one thing, the lungs sing another,
our bodies were made for sun and sweet clover

not these plains of dust stretching forever,
on which we would lie if our lines should sever

or our helmets open, like metallic clams,
our faces the pearls, should stout hinges jam.

But let heart be strong! Let will rule the day!
Feeble trembling never shall stand in our way!

Our strides shall mark out this new orb
let fear evaporate, let brain absorb

all that can will be taken, all the moon's wiles
shall be unveiled, mined, and laid in sweet piles

and shipped back to England in many more trains;
more blood flowing through Trade's 'normous veins.

Our moon may prove to be another Bombay,
or Peking, or Manchester, and who shall say nay?

But such delights lie in the Future's closed book;
time for we pilgrims to have the first look.

***

Cautiously we moved, as the slightest leap,
could propel us forward and up like Barbary sheep.

Seven league boots may still be a dream
but seven yard strides were easy, it seems.

I heard a young man recite something 'bout apples
and Newton, who with gravity grappled,

and how his father would love to be here,
a man whose life (he murmured) burned as a meteor

and see this quiet beauty, its undefiled delight,
spinning though space and reflecting the light.

'Twas hard to hear, though our masks were equipped
with devices for speech, we all seemed to lisp.

I turned to tell him that here apples were bubbles
but received rather short shrift for my troubles.

He quickly departed, and, as he walked away
I noticed his small height, and his hips' sweet sway

'Tis she! I thought. A woman walks with us, out of the ship!
Her father should practise more stewardship.

Exploration is not for girl, woman or maid –
'tis not Man but God who such distinctions made.

But I hastened onwards, to see the sights planned,
and set up by the Captain's brave servant band.

What delights appeared over the next hundred feet,
first the flag that flies over Her Majesty's fleet

though the lack of a wind made the ensign not flap,
'twas fixed with some sticks by a practical chap.

Then statues representing our Empire eternal,
the extent of civilisation, from Bombay to Balmoral

(or in truth vice versa, for London's the centre
of all that's enlightened, and capital's great venture

at placing a belt of gold around the equator –
in the museum of wealth it's the only curator,

exhibiting machinery, boats, guns, precious woods
cotton, tea, wool, opium, and innumerable goods

and the skills of management and book-keeping
banking, accounting and general good teaching).

In each work an Englishman was instructing a native
in agriculture, science, or just how to pray with

the right attitude, to, of course, the right God.
Also, shoes were being presented to the unshod.

'Twas a panoply of progress, a proud declaration
of the achievements of the world's foremost nation.

How my heart swelled! My tears fogged my helmet.
Such a dear sight I shall never forget.

I fear our young Jane Gordon was quite overcome,
for she spun on her heel and soon she was gone.

So I doubt that she saw the light-hearted sight
of gnomes, fairies, elves and other such sprites

bound to provide amusement to all who should see them.
Too late for her, slight-hearted femme!

So amusing, the industrious gnomes displayed,
working with rakes, ladders and spades!

***

That evening I heard her talk with the Captain
and was shocked to hear her speak in high dudgeon.

She banged her fair fist on a small table
(fortunately it was attached and quite stable).

'Mathematics being used for exploration is one thing
But not for a vulgarity worthy of Elgin,

who desecrated beauty with no right at all.
Unthinking jingoism must always appal.

I would never be party to such a display
the moon belongs to no-one, and so shall it stay!'

Poor dear was obviously quite overcome
as she left the salon at full near a run.

I tried to greet her, but none was she having.
We saw her no more; she stayed to her cabin.

***

In searching for her one night (or so I assume)
while yet we were docked by the side of the moon

I heard strange rustling from behind a locked door
and words in a language I'd not heard before,

a succession of clicks and loud guttural cries,
that scarce can have come from under our skies

but rather from elsewhere, yes, another planet –
ashamed to say that it caused me to panic.

The door began opening. I fell pregnant with dread.
If its voice were evil, who knew how it fed?

I ran to my cabin, quite unmanned and weak
at the thought of what could possibly speak

such hideous words, if words they indeed were,
more like an insect's clicks, and foul flies' wings' whirr,

and dog's bark distorted as if through a bell,
surely a noise from a new-opened Hell?

After myself I upbraided, and to that cabin returned.
I found it open, empty, and thus never learned

who or what made the strange monstrous sounds.
Still in my dreams the noises rebound,

and I wake and feel ill, and sleep runs away,
I wait through the night for another long day.

The door is always opening, creaking.
Their voices, hideous, always speaking.

***

It has been said by those who know not
that the whole venture was merely a plot,

that we never left earth at all, but were prey to magicians,
or mesmerists, aided by fiendish physicians,

that a device was able to project moons onto walls.
Rubbish! say I, such ignorance appals.

No drug entered my head or my veins,
my faculties were set, neither waxed nor waned.

I felt the tracks, saw the view, felt the thrust.
I touched the statues, gnomes, sang, and tasted the dust.

***

It's true that no-one has gone back again.
Foul sabotage is the reason! For when

the train-ship docked back home, bombs soon blew
her to pieces; and the plans and the crew

were either lost or abducted, the Captain included.
Total disaster, you may say, could be averted

if the Sage behind the project were identified, persuaded,
that Britain's great lunar mission must be prosecuted

that he must now come forward, and do his duty!
Expansive ventures manifest true beauty.

Crude Luddites must never control our quest!
We must go further, we must do our best.

The tracks were blown, they stretched down like wings
That dear Salisbury should witness such things!

And the train-ship itself was totally lost,
like a ship on the sea all scuppered and tossed.

The man set to guard her, my old servant Jim,
was coshed and unconscious and saw not a thing.

Time will tell if the steam-engine rebirths
or whether we're stuck with just the one earth.

***

I saw her, I'm sure, just once, boarding a yacht
I called out 'Jane!' but she heard me not.

It was down at the Isle of Wight
when her visage hove into sight.

(My eyes are, it's true, now growing quite dim,
but I thought I saw also my Scots servant Jim.)

I called out again, but the breeze stole my words.
They winged away with the white feckless birds.

She heard me not, and The Ada pulled away.
At night she walks still, with unforgettable sway.

***

Fair nymph! She went where no other woman has gone
and stole a heart from a man, now old and alone,

but visited at night by both the lovely and hideous,
one near an angel, the other Space's Cerberus.

The End

'(although the firm's offices are on The Strand).' The Strand may seem an odd place for a steam-space-travel firm to have its offices, unless the venture was based in a fashionable private house.

'£10,000' This equates to approximately £1,200,000 in today's money (well over AUD2,000,000) as of late 2019. This is substantially more than the cost of a ticket for a flight on Virgin Galactic, at approximately USD250,000. However, there is admittedly no promise of a visit to the moon on these flights.

'Richard Dadd' (1817-1886) a noted painter of supernatural and 'orientalist' themes spent most of his life in psychiatric hospitals. His best-known work, *The Fairy Feller's Master-Stroke*, hangs in The Tate, London.

'Charles and John Deane.' The Deane brothers (1796-1848 and 1800-1884) invented the diving helmet, which they developed from an earlier smoke helmet.

'a vulgarity worth of Elgin' Thomas Bruce, 7th Earl of Elgin and 11th Earl of Kincardine (1766-1841) removed sculptures and friezes from Greece's Parthenon. They are now in the British Museum. Byron wrote about this act in *Childe Harold's Pilgrimage*:

> Dull is the eye that will not weep to see
> Thy walls defaced, thy mouldering shrines removed
> By British hands, which it had best behoved
> To guard those relics ne'er to be restored...
> – (Canto XV)

'The Ada' This is the most explicit clue that the only woman on the voyage, and, perhaps, the unknown 'Sage' behind the expedition was Ada Lovelace. Born as the Hon. Augusta Ada Byron, she was a mathematician, and '[s]he was the first to recognise that the machine had applications beyond pure calculation, and published the first algorithm intended to be carried out by such a machine. As a result, she is sometimes regarded as the first to recognise the full potential of a computing machine and as one of the first computer programmers.' (Wikipedia). She died at the age of 36, the same age as her father, whose epigraph opens this strange work.

www.ingramcontent.com/pod-product-compliance
Ingram Content Group Australia Pty Ltd
76 Discovery Rd, Dandenong South VIC 3175, AU
AUHW021820210826
431587AU00001B/5